D0653191

For (Hugless) Doug, Liella, Christina and Alessia,
with hugs for Monika and Luka.
www.huglessdouglas.co.uk
www.davidmelling.co.uk

Happy Birthday, Hugless Douglas!

David Melling

A division of
Hachette Children's Books

One very special day, Douglas was waiting for his friends.

And while he waited he blew up **LOTS** of balloons. 'Where are they?' he sighed.

'HAPPY BIRTHDAY, DOUGLAS!'

his friends cried as they
burst through the door.
Douglas had so many
presents, he lined
them up in a row.
He was just about to start
opening them when...

'SURPRISE!'

It was Douglas's twin cousins, Felix and Mash, and the

BIGGEST PRESENT

he had ever seen!

'Oooh!' said Douglas.

'Wow, look at all these **PRESENTS!**' said the twins. 'Let's open them!' Felix and Mash bustled past Douglas and helped themselves. 'Oh,' said Douglas. He liked opening presents.

The room was soon a **BIRTHDAY MESS!**

'Don't forget the big one from us,' giggled the twins. 'It's a doctor's trolley.'

Before Douglas could say thank you, they tore open the wrapping.

'Oh,' said Douglas again. He was really looking forward to doing that himself. 'I want to play outside,' he said, a little sadly.

But Douglas wasn't any happier outside. He felt left out while everyone watched Felix and Mash push and pull the trolley about.

'IT'S **MY** BIRTHDAY!'
he said and grabbed his
new pogo stick.
'Watch me bounce.'

'OWWW!' cried Douglas. 'My leg hurts. And my new pogo stick is broken. This is my worst birthday ever!'

Poor Douglas sat up
and blew his nose.
'I feel a bit dizzy,' he sniffed.

The twins clambered onto the doctor's trolley.

'NEE-NAW... NEE-NAW.

Felix and Mash to the rescue!'

'It's not that bad,' said Douglas quietly.

'Nonsense!' said Rabbit.

'We'll look after you.'

Douglas tried to stand, with a little help.
But it was no good.
'Hmm,' said Rabbit, 'I have an idea.'

‘Now then,’ said Doctor Rabbit,
‘shhh everyone. I need to listen for
important noises with this listening straw.’

‘Hmm. Yes… oh, yes, just as
I thought,’ frowned Doctor Rabbit.
‘Douglas, you’ve hurt your leg.
And it’s definitely this one,’
she said, pointing.

Felix and Mash unravelled the **BIRTHDAY BANDAGES** and passed them around. 'We should practise bandage-wrapping before we help Douglas,' said Doctor Rabbit.

'Yes, please,' Douglas agreed.

'It's a bit like wrapping presents, isn't it?' said Douglas.
'Where's Hedgehog?'
'Here,' came a muffled voice. 'I'm fine, thank you!'

Douglas was a little wobbly, so the twins found two long sticks and helped him stand. ‘We’re sorry you hurt your leg,’ said Felix.

Douglas smiled. ‘Come on, let’s all go home.’

When they arrived there was one more surprise waiting for Douglas. It was a **BIRTHDAY TEA PARTY!**

After Cow's cake-and-ballooon-sandwiches Douglas felt much better. 'Time to play Doctors again!' he said.

Luckily, there were enough
bandages for everyone. Douglas laughed,

'This is My Best Birthday Ever!'

Surprise present
Balloons
Birthday hug
Birthday bunting
Party hats

Birthday cake

Party twirl

Party tricks

Party poppers

Happy Birthday, Hugless Douglas!
by David Melling

First published in 2014 by Hodder Children's Books

Hodder Children's Books
338 Euston Road
London NW1 3BH

Hodder Children's Books Australia
Level 17/207 Kent Street
Sydney NSW 2000

A catalogue record of this book is
available from the British Library.

ISBN: 978 1 444 91326 2
10 9 8 7 6 5 4 3 2 1

Printed in China

Hodder Children's Books
is a division of Hachette
Children's Books.
An Hachette UK Company.

www.hachette.co.uk